GOD VS. DEVIL

Written by

Devansh Arora

TANEESHA
PUBLISHING

ISBN : 9788169244978
Edition : First, March 2026
Title : God Vs. Devil
Author : Devansh Arora

Published by

TANEESHA PUBLISHING

An Imprint of **Taneesha and Prachi NextGen Publication**

Registered Address: Plot No. 48, Khasra No. 646, Road No. 2,
Suman Nagar, Bahadarabad, Haridwar, Uttarakhand – 249402, India
Website : www.samantpublishing.com
E-mail : support@tpnextpub.com
Phone : +91 9760418103

Printed by :
Manipal Technologies Limited, Bengaluru - 560001, Karnataka

Table of Content

Chapter One

Where Faith Ends

The wall had once been white. Perhaps even proud. Now it stood flushed. Upon its surface, carved not written, was a number. The digits had been etched with impatience, almost desperation.

It was a number to contact a witch. Vinny stopped.

She had not meant to stop. Her arms were burdened with market poly bags; coriander leaves peeked out like fragile witnesses, and a bottle of cooking oil tapped gently against her thigh with each step. She had meant to pass by. She had meant to remain a rational woman.

But the eyes betray before the mind does. They lingered on the carving.

The number seemed less an invitation and more a temptation. For months she had trained herself not to look at children too long. Not to count their laughter. Not to feel that sharp, humiliating emptiness that arises when one realizes that destiny has withheld something elemental.

Later that evening, she stood by the railing of the park, watching children running over grass that did not belong to them but was nonetheless claimed with shrieks of joy. A small boy stumbled. His mother rushed forward. Vinny felt something tighten in her chest. It was not pain, but yearning.

At dinner, the domestic ritual unfolded.

"What did you buy at the mall today?" Gauransh asked casually.

"Some dresses. Perfume. And a wristwatch."

He paused. "Wristwatch? I hope it's not the one you always wanted to buy."

She did not shake her head.

The silence that followed was arithmetic. "That watch was forty-six thousand!"

She shrugged. "I'm earning now."

There are truths that sound like rebellion even when spoken calmly. She had rejoined school only two months ago. The salary was modest. The numbers did not justify the purchase. But the purchase was not about time.

It was about control.

"Save money for what?" she said. "It's not as if we're waiting for someone to grow up…to send them to a good school."

The sentence detonated softly. It did not shout; it simply existed. Gauransh had no answer. How does one argue against absence?

That night, as her husband slept, Vinny lay awake. She was weighing a decision.

After some time, she slipped into her slippers and stepped into the hall.

The number from the wall had followed her home. She dialed it.

Far away, in a dim chamber where pillar candles trembled like obedient servants, a woman was fastening pins into a puppet's torso with delicate concentration. Jewel looked too beautiful to be called a witch without irony.

She lifted her eyes in irritation when the phone rang. She rejected the call.

The phone rang again.

Annoyance sharpened into curiosity. "Hello. Ha."

The caller responded with her story.

A smile unfolded across Jewel's lips. It was slow, knowing, almost affectionate toward human weakness.

Vinny cleaned her old mountain bike in the lawn the next morning. Dirt dissolved under the pipe's water. The bicycle began to shine. Sweat formed along her fair skin, glistening under the sun.

"Since when did you start cycling again?" Gauransh asked. She smiled vaguely.

Gauransh mistook restoration for a hobby.

He failed to understand that she was preparing herself for a movement, a secrecy, a path that required distance.

Her legs moved in steady rhythm, cutting through the mountain air as she pedaled upward in blue shorts, the fabric catching light between shadowed turns of the road. The road bent and curved through valleys where pine forests whispered and a distant river glimmered.

And at the end of the winding ascent stood the structure. A cubical house with a triangular roof. Too symmetrical to feel natural. A fence of wooden stakes surrounded it. The

fence was so low that even a dwarf could clamber over it. It was not meant to keep people out.

Vinny parked her bike outside.

She walked to the door and knocked.

Inside the unworldly house, the hall smelled faintly of dried herbs and something metallic beneath it.

Jewel appeared from the kitchen carrying two cups of tea. Steam rose slowly, twisting like spirits escaping porcelain prisons. She placed one before Vinny and then sat down across from her.

"Your name is very beautiful. Jewel."

"Thank you. A few years ago I went to France. For studies. There I met a woman. Over time we became close friends…and eventually she told me her secret. She was a witch."

Jewel took a slow sip of tea.

"I found her profession…interesting. So I became part of her coven. After my first ritual succeeded, they gave me this name."

"Oh."

Jewel reached into her pocket and pulled out a pack of cigarettes.

She extended it forward. "Cigarette?"

"No, thank you. I don't smoke."

Jewel tilted her head. "Because it's bad for health?"

Vinny shook her head.

"It's not about health. I just don't understand the concept. It doesn't even get you high. So what's the point?"

A small smile appeared on Jewel's lips. "Do you like marijuana?"

Vinny chuckled.

"No. I only drink. That too occasionally. Once or twice a month."

Jewel nodded. Lit the cigarette.

The first drag seemed almost ceremonial.

Smoke curled upward, weaving between them like a silent third participant in the conversation.

Then her tone shifted. It became slower.

Heavier.

"God refused to bless you with a child. They will not help you. But the Devil…the Devil always helps those who are willing."

Vinny's fingers tightened around her cup.

Jewel stood and walked toward the window. Outside, a hilltop town rested.

"Tell your husband you are staying here tonight," Jewel continued. "Understanding our business takes time."

Night settled over the house.

A bonfire burned between Jewel and Vinny, its flames rising and collapsing in restless shapes. Sparks drifted upward and disappeared into the black sky.

Vinny's phone screen dimmed as she locked it.

"I told Gauransh I'm staying with a friend tonight." "He doesn't suspect you?"

"No."

"That means he truly loves you. I just hope the truth doesn't break his heart one day."

"I'm never going to tell him the truth." Jewel's eyes reflected the firelight.

"When the time comes…you may not have a choice." "Why?"

For a moment, only the crackling fire answered. Then Jewel leaned forward.

"God created laws for the Human World. Among them, the most important is the Law of Nature. According to it, humans must not use magic. Magic in the Human World is banned. For humans. For demons. Even for angels."

Vinny swallowed the doctrine.

"So the moment we use magic…we become criminals in God's eyes?"

"Yes."

"And if we're caught?"

Jewel's gaze lifted toward the dark sky.

"To maintain law and order, God deployed angels in the Human World. Patrolling Angels. Their purpose is simple. To hunt and eliminate those who violate the Law of Nature."

A slow exhale of smoke left her lips. "Fortunately, I have never been caught."

The fire shifted violently as a gust of wind struck it. Vinny's voice trembled slightly.

"After this ritual…which will impregnate me, will they come after me too?"

"Yes."

"And my child?" "Yes."

The word landed like a stone. "What would be my child's fault?" Jewel looked almost amused.

"You've heard the saying - the apple doesn't fall far from the tree. Consider it something like that."

Vinny stared into the flames, watching shapes form and dissolve.

"What precautions can we take?" Jewel's tone grew clinical now.

"Your child will be born with a Proximity Fuse."

Vinny frowned.

"What does that mean?"

"It means he cannot form deep bonds with those who have not broken the Law of Nature. He cannot interact freely. He cannot love freely. He will exist in this world without belonging to it."

The wind pressed harder against the solids in proximity.

"He will enter the Human World without God's permission," Jewel continued. "Which means he will live here like an illegal immigrant - always present, never accepted."

"And if he breaks that rule?"

"The Proximity Fuse activates. The Protection Spell placed by the Devil will explode. The angels will trace him."

She paused.

"And they will trace us."

Morning returned with deceptive gentleness.

Sunlight poured over hills blanketed in flowers and wild shrubs. The wind was fresh and innocent, almost newborn in its clarity.

Vinny and Jewel walked along a narrow path carved into the hillside.

"Even now," Jewel said calmly, "you can back out. Don't lose your husband in pursuit of a child."

Vinny's expression hardened.

"I'm about to shake hands with the Devil. I should get used to taking risks."

She looked ahead.

"And if Gauransh's love is truly real, he won't leave me."

Jewel smiled. "Words of wisdom."

Vinny stopped walking.

"Tell me what I have to do." A pause.

"Human sacrifice."

Vinny froze. "What!?"

Jewel shrugged lightly, as though discussing grocery lists. "You must offer a human life."

"You said that so casually! Isn't there another way?"

"This ritual is based on magical replacement," Jewel explained. "For someone to arrive…someone must depart."

Vinny felt nausea rise in her throat. "How can I kill someone?"

Jewel began walking again.

"Shortcuts are easy to walk on," she said without looking back. "But difficult to discover. Go back to your God if you wish. Pray. Beg. The Devil's path is not for you."

Vinny remained still long after Jewel disappeared ahead.

Later, inside the hall, Jewel sat smoking at the table. Vinny entered quietly and sat beside her.

Silence stretched between them. Then -

"Who will we sacrifice?"

Jewel's eyes gleamed. Her energy shifted instantly. It revived, became electric.

"Someone God loves. A selfless human. Someone who helps others without expecting reward or publicity."

"And how do we find such a person?"

Jewel stood.

"Draw the curtains."

The room darkened.

Jewel placed a Scrying Ball at the center of the table. Its surface was reflective, too reflective.

She closed her eyes. And began to chant.

The language was ancient. Enochian. Harsh syllables that did not belong to the modern tongue. A language created in the sixteenth century by occultists John Dee and Edward Kelley. It is said to be the speech of angels.

But tonight, it did not sound angelic. It sounded summoned.

The temperature dropped.

The crystal surface began to shimmer. Something was forming within it.

And for the first time, Vinny wondered not whether this was evil.

Their plan initiated with Vinny going to a salon. The scent of talcum powder, shaving cream, and cheap cologne hung in the air. A fan rotated lazily overhead.

She walked straight to the hairdresser.

"Samarth comes here for his haircuts, doesn't he?" The man nodded cautiously. "Yes."

"I need a lock of his hair." The scissors paused mid-air. "And one drop of his blood."

The hairdresser blinked, confused. "I don't understand."

Vinny slowly removed a thick band of currency from her handbag. Crisp notes. Neatly stacked.

"You don't need to understand. I've heard the rent of this shop is suffocating you. This should cover the next five months."

The hairdresser's eyes lowered to the money. Then rose to her face. Then lowered again.

The next day, a teenage boy sat in the chair patiently, as his hair got trimmed.

A slight slip of the blade.

A sharp intake of breath from the boy.

"Oh, sorry beta," the hairdresser said quickly, pressing tissue against the shallow cut near his neckline. "Just a small nick."

A dot of red stained the white paper.

Moments later, as hair fell to the floor in soft clumps, the hairdresser discreetly collected what she had asked for.

Jewel and Vinny sat in a corner booth of a café. The hum of coffee machines masked their conversation.

"Now we have Samarth's hair and blood," Vinny said. "What happens next?"

Jewel stirred her tea calmly.

"I need to gather materials for the ritual. It will take a week. I'll call you when it's time. Give Gauransh another excuse and come."

Vinny nodded.

"And when the ritual is complete?"

"A demonic legion will be assigned to Samarth." She spoke the word with precision.

"In demonology, a legion refers to a structured army of demons. They will not kill him immediately. They will gradually break him. Make him lose his will to live. And the day he finally gives up, they will extract his soul. Take it to Hell."

A pause.

"And the exchange will be complete."

Chapter Two

The Desire to Belong

There are places in every town that exist unofficially. Like hidden smoking corners behind roadside stalls.

One such place sheltered a tall, slender young man. His name was Tamas.

His phone rang.

He picked it up lazily.

"Send me the list on message. I'll get whatever you need."

Later, he dragged a trolley through a departmental store, scanning shelves mechanically.

Until he saw her.

A store employee arranging packaged goods. Her name badge read Eashna.

He slowed down without realizing.

There was something about her. A contained story. He kept walking gradually, but his mind stayed behind.

By now, Vinny had aged.

Time had carved fine lines into her once-smooth face. Her hair had thinned. Her eyes carried history.

She sat across from Tamas at a dining table.

"I like her," he said. "I don't know why, but I want to know her story. I want to be part of it."

"Control your desires. Or we both die."

"I'm not afraid of dying," he replied. "I've only restrained myself because of you."

"How many times will we have this discussion, Tamas? How long will it take you to accept reality?"

He laughed softly, but it sounded hollow.

"Whenever I try to accept reality instead of fighting it, strange thoughts come to me. Dangerous thoughts."

"What thoughts?"

"That having a child is wrong. Someone is born without consent. No one asks if they want to come into this world. And once here, they can't even leave freely. Even suicide is declared a crime."

Vinny stared at him sharply.

"Are you thinking about killing yourself?"

"I don't know. I just can't bear this loneliness anymore." "You have Damian."

"He's a demon. I need a human."

Tamas sat in the passenger seat of a moving car beside a sharply dressed gentleman in a suit.

"Why do demons always wear suits?" Tamas asked.

"We consider ourselves gentlemen," Damian replied. "God refuses to acknowledge that. So we mock him by dressing the part."

"That logic makes no sense."

"If you think deeply enough," Damian said, "even a fool's words begin to sound logical."

"And on what basis do you call yourselves gentlemen?"

Damian smiled.

"We never possess a human without permission."

Tamas laughed bitterly. "Why would anyone give permission?"

"We make them desperate enough to ask for it," Damian said plainly.

"Well," Tamas said sarcastically, lighting two cigarettes, "that's very gentlemanly of you."

"Thank you."

Smoke filled the car.

"I like a girl," Tamas admitted. "Who?"

"She works in a departmental store."

Damian's expression darkened.

"You know the consequences of loving her."

"Oh please. I've seen the movies. She'll leave me one day, and I'll destroy myself. Classic."

"I'm not talking about cinematic consequences," Damian said coldly. "If you form a bond with her, the Proximity Fuse activates."

Tamas' jaw tightened. "And then?"

"According to God's designed chronology, angels will first eliminate the witch. Then Vinny. And then you."

"I don't care anymore," Tamas said. "I want to know what it feels like to have a friend. A girlfriend. A social circle. The risk is worth it."

"It's not a risk," Damian snapped. "It's suicide. You cannot fight angels. Do you have any idea how powerful they are?"

Tamas looked out the window.

"Once, five countries attacked Israel together. No one thought it would survive. But today it stands strong."

Damian stared at him.

"You're comparing yourself - one individual - to an entire nation?"

"It's about spirit," Tamas replied. "Not size." "I'd still call it delusion."

"What do you want then? That I spend my entire life alone?"

Damian's voice softened.

"I care for you. I don't want you killed."

Tamas flicked the cigarette butt out of the window. "One question."

"What?"

"What are my chances?"

Damian exhaled slowly.

"It would be like placing a single bet on zero in a game of roulette."

A single bulb swung gently in the darkness, its yellow light forming a trembling circle over a wooden table.

Beyond that circle, nothing existed.

Two women sat across from each other in white gowns that glowed faintly under the light. Their makeup was heavy, deliberately excessive, as if beauty itself were armor. Their fingers moved with calculated ease over a deck of cards.

Vanessa struck the table and revealed her hand. A straight.

Nancy's brows lifted slightly. "Impressive."

Vanessa leaned back with satisfaction. "I knew I'd win today."

"How?"

Vanessa smiled as though revealing divine wisdom.

"This morning you slipped in the bathroom. Then your lunch order turned out terrible. And your favorite cigarette brand was out of stock."

She tapped the table softly.

"Those weren't coincidences. They were signals." She gathered the cards lazily.

"Signals that you shouldn't have played today."

Nancy's lips curved. "I did notice them." "Then why did you still play?"

Nancy's eyes sharpened.

"Because winning feels best when all the odds are against you."

She placed her cards down. A straight flush of hearts.

Vanessa froze. "What the-?"

"I don't believe in luck," Nancy said confidently. "I believe in myself."

"You used your psychic abilities," Vanessa accused. "You had to."

Nancy reached for a cigarette and lit it, the flame briefly illuminating her eyes.

"Magic is restricted in the Human World. I'm not becoming an outlaw just to win a small game."

Vanessa frowned. "I can't keep losing every day."

Nancy exhaled smoke slowly.

"Years ago, a legion ambushed Anna and me. Seven of them. Two of us."

The bulb above them flickered once. "They outnumbered us. Brutally." She paused.

"Other angels think I survived because of luck." Her gaze hardened.

"But luck doesn't save you in battle. Belief does." She tapped ash into a tray.

"That day, I knew I would walk away alive." Her phone began to ring.

Nancy answered without breaking eye contact with Vanessa. "Yes."

A pause.

"Alright. We'll leave tomorrow." She disconnected.

"Who was it?"

"A secret informer from our association. He located the husband of a convict."

Elsewhere, Vinny held her phone tightly against her ear. "So you're still not seeing anyone?" she asked anxiously.

"No," Gauransh replied.

"Then why don't you come back?"

"I'm sorry to say this…but I can't live with a murderer."

The word struck deeper than accusation.

Vinny's voice wounded. "You don't want to return to me. You don't want to start over with someone else. What exactly do you want?"

His answer came slowly.

"I want to remain disconnected from this world. As much as I can."

"But why?"

A long breath passed through the receiver.

"Because if you can become a terrible person…then anyone can."

The sentence cut cleanly.

Vinny felt something inside her fracture. Without another word, she disconnected the call.

A door stood slightly ajar.

A thin line of darkness bled through it. Tamas stepped inside.

Or rather his shadow did first.

It slid across the floor like spilled ink before his body followed.

He reached for a candle resting near the wall and lit it with trembling fingers. The flame flickered wildly, as if resisting the room.

Light revealed fragments.

Symbols scratched into the floor. Melted wax hardened in chaotic rivers. Ash scattered in imperfect circles.

A metallic smell still lingered. He took another cautious step.

A broken bowl lay overturned. Dried residue clung to its edges. Strange markings. The place had witnessed something. Not recently. But intensely.

His breath caught.

The thin veil of normalcy tore in that moment. He understood.

A ritual had been performed here. Something had been invited.

Or released.

He gasped and woke up. Tamas sat upright in his bed, sweat clinging to his neck.

Just a dream.

Only a dream.

Yet his heart refused to slow.

Later,

He sat at a small table in a café, slurping noodles with careless ease, as if nothing haunted him.

Damian arrived moments later and slid into the seat opposite him, impeccably dressed as always.

"How many times have I told you not to call me to restaurants?" Damian said, mildly irritated.

Tamas grinned. "Well, God is merciful. As punishment, he only restricted demons from eating. Not drinking. Not smoking."

Damian leaned slightly closer to the bowl, inhaling deeply. "He shouldn't have restricted eating. At least not fried food. Smell that."

"Then eat some," Tamas teased. "If you're ready to die."

Damian's eyes narrowed.

"Which cuisine is the best to die for?"

"I was joking," Tamas laughed. "Why would you want to die such a dishonorable death? What would your dimension's newspaper say? Damian died because he ate something fried?"

Damian stared at him.

"Very amusing. Why did you call me?"

Tamas wiped his mouth.

"I'm approaching her this evening." "Her?"

"The girl from the departmental store."

"Are you certain? Think once more. In chasing her, you may lose what little you still have."

"I have nothing to lose."

"You know that before we possess a human, we examine their aura. Their orientation toward life. Whether their approach is positive or negative."

"Why does that matter?"

"Because God dislikes those who reject the gift of life. Negativity is indirectly a denial of existence. Such humans are easier to possess."

He paused.

"But after possession…they often realize the value of life too late."

Tamas' expression hardened.

"What exactly are you trying to say?"

"Perhaps what you think is insufficient…might already be enough."

Tamas shook his head.

"It doesn't matter what you say. I've made up my mind."

Damian sighed.

"Very well. I'll inform the Devil." "About what?"

"That the task I failed to accomplish years ago…you now intend to attempt."

Tamas frowned. "What task?"

Damian's voice lowered.

"My companions and I once attempted to kill a couple of angels."

Silence swallowed the table. "We failed."

The words carried weight.

And in that moment, Tamas realized he wasn't merely risking love.

He was stepping into a war that even demons had once lost.

Damian drove back alone.

The city blurred past his windshield, but his mind was not in the present. It reminisced about his encounter with the angels he failed to kill.

Chapter Three

Finding Life At The Suicide Door

Six other demons sat with Damian in a strange hall. They looked tense, hungry for glory. Damian remembered his own voice. It was sharper, younger, fueled by ambition.

"Eight years," he said. "Eight years since an angel fell by our hands. The reason is clear. In direct combat, they are superior. But if our numbers exceed theirs," he continued, "we can overpower them. And today is our opportunity. They don't know we're coming. We cannot lose this chance at any cost."

One of the demons responded viciously. "We're going to make the Devil proud tonight."

"We have to. At any cost. This time it's either do or die!"

The legion entered the hotel building as if they belonged there. Polished marble floors. Muted lighting. The scent of artificial lavender drifting through conditioned air.

At the reception desk, a young woman looked up politely. "Good evening, sir."

Damian smiled with effortless civility. "Could you tell us which floor the restaurant is on?"

"Fourth floor, sir." "Thank you."

Seven demons walked toward the elevators like businessmen heading to dinner. But beneath their coats, daggers remained unsheathed.

The fourth-floor corridor was silent. Their footsteps echoed against carpeted flooring. Damian raised his hand, signaling them to stop outside a particular room.

He rang the bell.

A woman opened the door.

She barely had time to register the strangers before Damian's blade flashed.

One swift motion.

Her throat opened like torn silk.

Blue fluid, luminous and unnatural, pulsed outward.

Her body collapsed and dissolved before it fully touched the ground.

Inside the room,

Nancy was tying her shoelaces. She froze.

Her partner.

Anna.

Gone.

The demons crossed the threshold one by one, surrounding her in a tightening circle.

Nancy rose slowly.

From beneath her coat, she drew her dagger. The fight erupted without warning.

Steel collided with steel.

Nancy moved like controlled lightning - precise, economical, devastating. She parried one blade, twisted another arm, drove her dagger upward beneath a ribcage.

Black fluid spilled from demonic wounds, thick and shadow- like.

One vanished. Then another. A third.

The room became chaos with shattered furniture, splintered glass and rage made physical.

Six demons fell. Six dissolved.

Damian attacked from behind. Once.

Twice.

Thrice.

His blade entered her body with deliberate force. Nancy staggered.

Her dagger slipped from her fingers.

She collapsed onto the blood-slicked floor.

Damian stood over her, breathing heavily, staring down at the angel who had annihilated his legion alone.

He crouched beside her.

Her breathing was uneven but her eyes burned fiercely. "What are you looking at?" she demanded.

"You destroyed my entire legion by yourself," he said. "I can't believe it."

A faint smirk curved her lips despite the blood at their corner. "I'm surprised you survived."

He chuckled.

Her voice sharpened with fury. "I want to kill you too."

Damian tilted his head. "For an angel, you don't sound like a saint at all."

He rose slowly.

"You know there's a quote by Buddha," he continued. "You will not be punished for your anger. You will be punished by your anger."

Nancy's eyes narrowed. "You're a demon. And you follow Lord Buddha?"

"No," he replied calmly. "But wisdom can be learned from anyone. Intelligence varies."

She let out a weak scoff. "Instead of finishing me, you're talking. What if I'm pretending? What if I get up and kill you? That would show your intelligence truly varies."

He grinned slightly. "Downwards, you mean?"

A pause lingered between them.

Then he said something neither of them expected. "I don't feel like killing you."

Nancy blinked, genuinely confused. "What?"

He studied her face - not with hatred, not with mockery. With admiration.

"Next Sunday," he said after a beat. "Five p.m. I'll be waiting at my favorite bar. Suicide Door."

Her breath caught. "Have you lost your mind? I'm an angel. You're a demon. If anyone finds out, we'll both be executed."

He ignored the warning entirely. "See you there."

He turned and walked toward the door. He did not look back.

Behind him, the bodies had vanished.

Only blue and black stains remained - proof that something impossible had occurred.

Nancy lay on the floor, bleeding, staring at the ceiling. An angel had survived.

A demon had spared her.

And somewhere beyond Heaven and Hell, for the very first time in history, a demon chose compassion and an angel learnt to doubt, and thus the universe began to rewrite its own scripture.

The bar pulsed with color.

Neon lights fractured into reds and blues, passing straight through Damian's body like stained glass through smoke.

Whiskey swirled lazily in his glass as he sat alone at a table.

He wasn't nervous.

Demons did not get nervous. But he was…aware.

The door opened. Nancy stepped inside.

She walked toward him and sat opposite without hesitation. "For a moment," Damian began, "I thought you wouldn't come." She said nothing.

"Then I remembered the way you fought us alone. Fear clearly isn't something you're familiar with."

"My opinion about you is different," she said straightforwardly. "I think you're a coward."

A flicker of amusement crossed his face.

"You're saying that in anger. We killed your partner. Otherwise you know very well that coming there alone wouldn't have been intelligent."

She nodded once. "Affirmative."

A small smile formed at the corner of his lips.

"So," he said smoothly, "what would you like? Whiskey? Wine? Rum? Vodka? Beer?"

"You didn't mention food." He laughed softly.

"LIIT," she said.

"I appreciate your choice," he replied, signaling the waiter.

Nancy lit a cigarette, studying him through the rising smoke.

"So…is this a date?"

"Of course."

"You're not afraid I might betray you? Kill you the moment I get a chance?"

"Kill me," he said casually. "But after this date. I think I deserve that much for sparing your life."

The honesty in his tone unsettled her more than arrogance would have.

A fragile truce.

After a moment, Damian spoke again.

"Humans go to Heaven or Hell after death. But God has never revealed where we go. You're close to him. Surely you know."

"I'm not that close," she replied. "His closest angel is Ash. His assistant."

"Then what do you think?" he asked. "Where do we go?"

She considered it carefully.

"There are only two possibilities. Either there's a third dimension beyond Heaven and Hell that only God knows about." She paused.

"Or something that frightens me even more."

"What?" "Nothingness."

Damian tilted his head.

"Nothingness could be a dimension in itself. A place where we can't see. Can't think. Can't feel."

She shook her head.

"I believe nothingness is the death of the soul."

The drinks arrived. She took a sip.

Her eyes softened slightly. “It’s perfect.”

“The quality here is always top-notch,” he said. “That’s why I wanted to meet you here.”

She leaned closer, voice lowering playfully. “Does that mean I can trust your choices for me?”

“Blindly!”

Damian returned from the memory. And his phone vibrated immediately.

“Nancy,” he answered, overwhelmed by the coincidence.

She stood at a petrol pump, wind tugging at her hair. “How are you?” she asked.

“Greater than the Great Wall of China.” She laughed. “How come?”

“I was thinking about us.” “Oh? What exactly?”

“Our first meeting.”

A soft exhale escaped her.

“That’s the most important chapter in my journal.” “What did you name it?”

“Finding Life at the Suicide Door.”

He smiled.

“That's creative.”

She laughed.

“I’m coming to your city.” “To see me?”

“No. For work. You know how busy God keeps me.” “Yes,” he said with disappointment. “I do.” “You’re free tonight?”

“For you? Always.”

“How sweet. Let's meet at Eight p.m. then.” “Where?”

She teased, “I’m coming to your city or you to mine?” He scratched his scalp.

“Right. I’ll text you a safe location.”

“Sure,” she said softly. A beat.

"I love you."

"I love you too."

Vinny hung freshly washed clothes along a wire in the lawn of her house

Tamas approached her. "Mom?"

"Yes?"

"How did you meet Dad?"

She looked mildly surprised. "Why this sudden curiosity?"

"I was thinking of keeping myself busy. Maybe start writing. Fictional stories. I need inspiration."

Her expression warmed.

"I appreciate that. It'll keep you away from overthinking." "So how did he propose?"

She smiled at the memory.

"He dressed up as my favorite cartoon character. Even learned to mimic his voice."

Tamas blinked. "He could've proposed directly."

"To impress someone," she said gently, "you have to make an effort."

Tamas expressed realization.

In the evening,

Damian stood before a breathtaking view of the city, cigarette between his fingers.

Nancy entered quietly behind him. "Been a long time, love."

He turned.

And in that very moment, he forgot war. Forgot rivalries. Forgot heaven. Forgot hell.

She ran into his arms. They kissed.

Later, they sat at the edge of an unfinished concrete structure, legs dangling above the sleeping city.

"How's your new partner?" he asked. "Vanessa?"

"Yes."

Nancy hesitated.

"I have mixed opinions." "Why?"

"She's competitive. That's not bad. I was the same once. But her competitiveness carries jealousy."

She stared at the skyline.

"And jealousy," she said softly, "is unpredictable."

Vanessa drove with rigid focus.

Nancy sat in the passenger seat, her feet resting casually on the dashboard.

"Why does God's informer always call you? He could call me too." Vanessa asked.

Nancy didn't look at her. "His job is to pass information to us. Whether he calls you or me - what difference does it make?"

"It wouldn't matter once or twice," Vanessa replied evenly. "But this has become a pattern now. Every time, it's you."

Nancy exhaled.

"It's because I'm more experienced. They consider me more competent."

"I'm a war veteran too."

"Yes," Nancy said calmly. "But a medical officer's role isn't as crucial as the frontline fighters."

Vanessa's hands tightened around the steering wheel. "God himself told me my contribution was significant."

Nancy turned slightly.

"A good leader appreciates every team member. There's nothing special about that."

Vanessa looked at her. "Really?"

Nancy nodded once.

Something dimmed in Vanessa's eyes.

She rolled down the window slightly and lit a cigarette. "I don't think she's vicious," Damian said.

Nancy frowned. "How can you be so sure?"

"She's expressing her jealousy," he replied. "If she wanted, she could've hidden it. At least she confronted you. That's honesty. She's not backstabbing you."

Nancy considered this. Then nodded slowly. "Hmm."

The wind moved through the skeletal structure of the building, carrying dust and distant traffic noise.

"By the way," Damian added lightly, "what songs are you listening to these days?"

"Mostly jazz."

"Really? Show me your playlist." "Why?"

"I don't think you're listening to jazz," he said, studying her. "You're lying."

She rolled her eyes. "Oh come on. Why would I lie?" "Then show me."

She hesitated.

Then surrendered with an exaggerated sigh. "Fine. I'm not listening to jazz."

"I knew it. So what are you listening to?" She looked away, embarrassed.

"Item numbers."

He blinked. "What's that?"

"A category of music. Obviously." "Yes, but about what?"

She struggled. "I don't know how to describe an item number."

"No problem," he said, pulling out his phone. "I'll check." She nudged him. "What's wrong with you?"

"Nothing. I'm just curious."

He read aloud from his screen:

"In Bollywood, an item number, also called an item song, refers to a musical number inserted into a film, often with little to no connection to the plot, primarily intended to be entertaining and marketable."

He burst out laughing.

"So that's why you were hiding it! Listening to those songs doesn't suit your personality."

"Whatever," she muttered, trying not to smile. The laughter faded.

Silence returned.

But this time it was heavier.

"How long," Damian asked with a crack in his heart, "are we going to keep meeting like this? Hiding. Running. I wish we were free."

Nancy stared at the horizon.

"I've started feeling like the Devil's offspring," she said. "I can't even be with the person I love."

"Then why not fall in love with an angel?" he teased lightly.

She turned to him. "I like bad boys."

He recoiled dramatically. "Yuck. How cliché!" She laughed.

The wind howled through the unfinished building. Far above,

Heaven watched.

Far below,

Hell calculated. And between them,

Two beings in love sat at the edge of the world, pretending the fall didn't exist.

Later, Damian walked her to her car. No grand speeches.

No promises.

Just a long look that said everything words couldn't. She stepped into the driver's seat.

The engine started.

The distance began again.

On the way back to Vanessa, Nancy's phone began to ring. The name flashing on the screen made her breath falter. Ash.

She answered.

"Good evening, Ash."

"Good evening," his calm voice replied. "How are you?" "I'm good.

What about you? And…how's God?"

There was a pause.

"God is…surprised," Ash said carefully. "To learn that you're having an affair with a demon."

The world seemed to tilt.

Nancy felt her fingers go cold against the steering wheel.

"A-according to whom?" she asked, perspiration forming along her temples.

"Does that matter now?" Ash replied.

Her heart pounded. "Yes. It does." She explains.

She hated the heaven's own ammunition store. Even parking outside irritated her.

"I hate coming here," she muttered.

"Why?" Anna asked from the passenger seat.

Inside the ammunition shop, a man stood polishing distinctive celestial daggers at the counter.

"Hi, Mandy," Nancy said flatly.

He removed his spectacles dramatically.

"Nancyyy," he breathed, overwhelmed. "It's been ages." "We met a week ago."

"For me," he sighed, "every day without you is a year." She sat down, unimpressed.

"You came to exchange your dagger last time. You only ever come here for work."

"I will always meet you professionally," she replied. "So please, give up on your surreal expectations."

Mandy's smile faded.

"You refuse to go on a date with me," he said quietly. "But loving a demon didn't seem wrong to you. I saw you. With that Devil's minion. Damian."

Anna's eyes widened. "What?"

Nancy turned sharply.

"Anna, he's obviously lying."

Mandy loses his cool.

"I could've taken a picture of you two. Sent it to God." "Why didn't you?" she asked, uninterested.

"Because I love you, Nancy," he said earnestly. "I can't watch you get executed."

She stared at him.

"I'm truly moved," she said coldly. "But I would rather be executed than be with you."

The words struck harder than any blade. "Am I that terrible?" he whispered.

"Yes," she replied simply. "Now can we discuss work? We heard you have new daggers in stock."

But as she left that day, a thought lingered. He could take revenge.

"Mandy could be lying," Nancy said into the phone. "He has motive."

"Mandy has nothing to do with this," Ash responded.

Her pulse quickened. "Then who told you?"

"I'm sorry. That's confidential."

A long silence followed. She swallowed.

"What punishment has God decided?"

Ash's voice softened.

"He loves you. You have always served with utmost dedication."

Her grip tightened.

"Therefore," he continued, "instead of the death penalty…he wishes to offer you a gift."

Nancy blinked. "A gift?"

"Our latest census shows very few Devil's offspring remain in the Human World. Some committed suicide. The rest were eliminated by patrolling angels. God has decided that if you successfully solve your currently assigned case…he will set you free."

Nancy couldn't breathe. "Free?"

"You and Damian," Ash clarified.

For a moment, she forgot how to speak. "Are you serious?"

"Yes. God is kind."

Tears blurred her vision. The impossible.

The forbidden.

The dream they never dared to hope for.

"Thank you, Ash," she whispered. "And.... thank God." "You're welcome."

The call ended.

Nancy looked hopeful. Freedom.

Not stolen. Not hidden. Earned.

But freedom came with a condition. A case.

A test.

And in Heaven,

Nothing was ever simple. Somewhere beyond sight, God watched.

And perhaps, for the first time, He was not watching with judgment. But curiosity.

Chapter Four

The Mother's Choice

Eashna stood behind the billing counter, scanning products. Beep.

Beep.

Beep.

Tamas pushed his trolley slowly toward her, carefully overfilled.

The more items, he thought, the longer the conversation. Genius.

He inhaled deeply, as if courage were oxygen, and stepped forward.

"Hi."

"Hello, sir," she replied politely. "How are you?"

"I'm good."

He nodded too enthusiastically.

"I buy all my household groceries from here. I'm a regular customer. You must've seen me before."

"I'm sorry, sir. I don't remember."

A small puncture in his confidence.

"Oh." He forced a smile. "By the way, I'm Tamas."

She didn't respond with her name. Silence.

"What's your name?" he asked gently.

She told him.

He repeated it slowly, tasting it.

"That's a beautiful name. What does it mean?"

Before she could answer, a stern-looking uncle leaned into the counter space.

"Is his bill done?"

Eashna stiffened. "Yes. Almost done."

The uncle shot Tamas a disapproving glare, a silent accusation, and the fragile bridge of conversation collapsed.

Tamas stepped aside. Opportunity interrupted.

Nancy and Vanessa stepped out of their car and approached the door of Gauransh's house.

The bell rang. The door opened.

"Hi," Nancy said. "I'm Nancy. And this is my partner, Vanessa."

"Hello?" he replied cautiously.

"We'd like to ask you a few questions." "Do I know you?"

"No."

"Then who are you?"

"We are patrolling angels."

A pause.

Then he exhaled, almost amused.

"I understand. Vinny sent you. This is some trick to get me back."

Nancy and Vanessa exchanged glances and laughed. "Maybe he thinks we're lying," Vanessa muttered. "Or maybe he just can't believe it," Nancy replied.

"What should we do?" Vanessa asked. Nancy tilted her head.

"I think we need to show him."

Vanessa stepped forward.

The punch came without warning.

Gauransh's body lifted off the ground and flung backward with inhuman force, crashing violently before landing in a heap.

Air left his lungs in a desperate gasp. The angels stepped inside.

Vanessa crouched near him. "Believe us now?"

He nodded weakly. "Good."

They sat at the dining table. Plates served.

An eerie civility.

"The sabji is good," Nancy commented.

"It is," Vanessa added. "Did your wife teach you to cook?" "This was made by my maid."

"Oh."

"You live alone then?" Nancy asked. "Yes."

"But your maid comes daily," Vanessa said casually. "Have you slept with her?"

He stiffened. "Excuse me?"

Nancy didn't soften it.

"You don't live with your wife. So you must satisfy yourself with someone else."

He scoffed, visibly uncomfortable.

"You came here to ask important questions."

Nancy leaned back.

"Correct. We need your wife's location." "Why?"

"You don't need the reason." "What if you want to harm her?" "We won't. We just want to talk."

He hesitated.

"She performed black magic. If God sent you, you're here to punish her."

"Why do you care?" Vanessa shot back. "You don't even love her."

His eyes flashed.

"Why would you assume that?"

"People in love stay together," Vanessa replied coolly. "They don't live apart."

He stood abruptly.

"I'm sorry. I can't help you. I don't know where she is."

Nancy's patience thinned.

"We're being polite because we expect cooperation."

He straightened, gathering what little pride he had left. "You said your name was Nancy."

"Yes."

"And you're Vanessa." "Yes."

He paused.

"Nancy and Vanessa, since you're being so nice to me, I'll respond nicely too."

Vanessa folded her arms. “Okay?”

“Go fuck yourselves.”

Nancy’s restraint shattered. “Grab him.”

Vanessa lunged.

Gauransh swung desperately, landing a weak punch. She caught his wrist mid-air and twisted it brutally.

A scream tore from him.

She lifted him and slammed him onto the supper table. Glass shattered.

A jagged shard pierced into his abdomen. He gasped.

The world blurred. Ceiling spinning.

Blood warm against his stomach.

Two silhouettes hovering above him.

“Is he going to die?” Vanessa asked.

Nancy observed him carefully. “No.”

Her voice was disturbingly calm. “No human dies without God’s will.”

Darkness crept into Gauransh’s vision.

Vinny sat on her bed, drinking whiskey when suddenly her body began to sweat uncontrollably. Her chest tightened, and she struggled to breathe.

Without warning, the window flew open as if pushed by an invisible force entering the room.

A strange, unseen presence overwhelmed her senses.

Within seconds, her eyes rolled back, and the cryptic entity put her into a deep, unnatural sleep.

Eashna stepped out of the store as another employee pulled the shutter down behind her. The market lights flickered one by one, and the street began to empty.

She had barely crossed the corner when a figure detached itself from behind a wall.

Tamas.

He had been waiting.

He followed her quietly, maintaining distance until she suddenly turned around.

Caught.

"Hello?" he said, pretending innocence.

"Are you following me mister?" she asked coldly. "Mister? Inside the store you were calling me sir."

"There, you were a customer," she replied. "Right now, you're a stalker. There's a difference."

"Look, I didn't mean to stalk you. I wanted to talk inside, but that uncle kept interrupting."

"What do you want to talk about?" "Nothing specific. Just…general stuff." "Why?"

"I want to befriend you."

She stared at him. "What if I don't want to be friends with you?"

Tamas had no answer.

"Stop following me," she said firmly.

Then she turned and resumed walking toward her hostel, leaving Tamas standing alone in the dim street, disappointment written all over his face.

The wind moved endlessly across the open pasture, bending the tall grass into silver waves.

Vinny and Gauransh wandered through the vastness, their footsteps soft against the earth, as though the ground itself were unsure whether to exist.

"May I ask you something?" Vinny glanced at him. "Sure."

"How does Tamas control himself? I mean, to not have a social life at all must be very difficult."

Vinny exhaled slowly. "He isn't doing anything extraordinary by controlling himself. We're both alone too. And you…you chose to be."

Gauransh laughed lightly. "Fair point."

Vinny's expression shifted, growing thoughtful. "But now it feels like the universe did not accept our separation."

"You mean we're trapped here permanently?"

"How am I supposed to know? I know as much as you do."

He smirked. "What if you performed black magic again just to get me back?"

Vinny stopped walking and looked at him firmly. "I have used black magic only once in my life. And you know when. So please."

Before he could reply, the distant thunder of hooves cut through the stillness.

A lone horseman emerged from the horizon, riding toward them through the mist. He wore a flowing white cloak and a pointed hat. Even from afar, something radiant surrounded him.

"Who is that?" Gauransh whispered. "I hope it's not an angel."

The rider approached and dismounted gracefully. He was impossibly handsome, and his presence magnetic, almost blinding.

"Hello, beautiful couple," he said warmly. "I must say, you both look wonderful together. You should not live apart."

Gauransh frowned. "How do you know we don't live together?" The man smiled faintly. "I know everything. About everyone." Vinny's voice hardened. "Who are you?"

He paused, as if even he found his answer amusing. "Sometimes I, too, struggle to believe it. But I am God. The entity chosen by this universe to administer Heaven, Hell, and the Human World."

The revelation struck them like lightning. A chill ran down their spines.

"My angels found your husband," God continued, looking at Gauransh. "They asked him for your location. He refused to tell them. So they killed him."

Vinny's breath trembled.

"His life is now in my hands," God said lightly. "I can let him live…or let him die. What should I do, Vinny?"

"Take me instead," she replied instantly.

"What nonsense are you saying?" Gauransh snapped.

"In my absence," she said to him softly, "you will take care of Tamas."

God raised an eyebrow. "Excuse me. I did not teleport your souls here to bargain. I have an offer. If you accept it, he lives. If you reject it, he dies."

"What kind of offer?"

"I created this dimension for the two of you. I hope you like it. You can stay here together. Forever. Just tell me where Tamas is."

"So you can kill him?"

"He will die anyway," God replied calmly. "If not today, then tomorrow. My patrolling angels will eventually find him."

"Then why ask me?"

"Because it has been too long," God said, his voice losing patience. "We have failed to catch him. I want the Devil's minions wiped out of the Human World as soon as possible, even if it means sparing a few criminals like you."

Vinny's eyes burned. "I'm sorry. Your offer is not good enough. A mother can give her life for her son. She cannot take his life for her own happiness."

God's smile vanished.

"As I said, you are in no position to bargain. I will ask one last time. Do you accept the offer?"

Vinny did not blink. "No."

"You have made the biggest mistake of your life," God said coldly. "Now you will realize that whom I cannot save, no one can save. You will pay for your sins very soon."

Vinny's grief turned into fury.

"You discriminate too. You let some be born rich, others poor. Some healthy, others burdened with illness. My friends became mothers but I could not. You created a broken, unfair world."

God's eyes darkened.

"If you find the Human World so terrible, imagine how Hell will feel. Prepare yourself, Vinny. The flames of hellfire await you."

And in the next instant, Vinny and Gauransh vanished. The echo of another horse galloping filled the pasture.

A second rider emerged, draped in a black cloak and hat. He stopped opposite God.

The two stared at one another like opposing forces painted into an eternal masterpiece.

The Devil smiled with excitement. "Hello, Father."

God's voice dripped with anger. "What are you doing here?"

"Nothing much. I was tracing the soul of my patron and happened to arrive." He lit a cigarette lazily. "You seem disappointed. Did Vinny reject your offer?"

"Enjoy this short-term victory while you can. The future of your patrons is not bright."

The Devil exhaled smoke into the air. "I respect your prediction. But I have a feeling…this time, you will lose."

God smiled slyly. "All the best."

They turned their horses and rode away in opposite directions.

Gauransh jolted awake for a brief second. Blood spilled from his mouth.

Then his body went limp.

Nancy rushed forward. "Check his pulse!"

Vanessa pressed her fingers against his neck. Her face drained of color.

"He's dead."

Nancy cursed under her breath. "Fuck." "What do we do now?"

Vanessa asked.

"I don't know." Nancy extended her hand. "Give me a cigarette."

Vanessa handed one over. Nancy lit it, sank into a chair, and scratched her scalp in frustration, smoke curling around her like a dark halo.

Vinny regained consciousness slowly, dizziness clouding her mind. She drank water in hurried gulps as fragments of memory returned.

Then the realization struck. Gauransh.

She rushed to Tamas and woke him up. They jumped into their car.

Inside, Tamas shoved the gear forward and drove recklessly toward Gauransh's residence.

The car screeched to a halt.

Vinny ran inside. Tamas followed close behind. She froze.

Gauransh lay on the floor, lifeless. A shard of glass protruded grotesquely from his stomach.

Her knees gave way.

She collapsed beside him, sobbing uncontrollably.

Tamas stared at the corpse for a long moment, a heavy sigh escaping him.

Then he wrapped his arms around his mother, holding her as she broke apart in his embrace.

Chapter Five

The Blade of Betrayal

Nancy returned to the underconstruction building. She sat on a concrete pedestal, her shoulders slumped, eyes distant.

Damian approached her. “Hi.”

“Hello,” she replied, her voice drained of life. “Why are you upset?”

“God knows about us.”

Damian let out a dry laugh. “The Devil knows too. And guess what? Thinking the enemy of their enemy is a friend, they’ve joined hands. Now both are coming to kill us. The good part? This centuries-old war might finally end with our deaths. So at least we won’t die for nothing.”

“I’m not joking, Damian.”

“If you’re not joking, then how are you still alive?”

“He spared me. Maybe he was pleased with my services and diligence.”

Damian paused, absorbing that. “Does that mean we can finally be together? If God has no issue, the angels won’t interfere too.”

“I wish life were that simple. God has assigned me a case. Only after I solve it can we be together.”

“Well, you’ll solve it,” he said confidently. “The lead we came here to interrogate…he’s dead.” “What did you need from him?”

“His wife’s address. She’s a convict.” “Why?”

“She performed black magic.” “Oh.”

Damian sat beside her and gently ran a reassuring hand along her back.

“Listen,” he said softly. “This time it’s not just professional. It’s personal. And I know you’ll finish it.”

After a moment, Nancy slowly nodded.

Damian drove back his car through the vacant streets of the sleeping town. His phone buzzed. He glanced at the screen and answered.

"Yes, Tamas?"

Tamas stepped out of Gauransh's house, his face pale. "Gauransh has been killed by angels."

Damian stiffened. "What? Why would angels kill him? He had nothing to do with Vinny's sin."

"I know. But he knew our address. They killed him because he refused to reveal it."

A flicker of realization passed through Damian's eyes. Nancy had come to interrogate Gauransh.

"Oh," he said, pretending ignorance. "What should we do now?" Tamas asked.

"Nothing. Leave the place immediately. I'll dispose of the body."

"Okay."

The call disconnected.

Nancy's earlier words echoed in his mind: "God has assigned me a case. Only after I solve it can we be together."

Damian's hands began to tremble, an overwhelming urge rising within him to light a cigarette.

Vinny lay stiff on her bed, as if staring at something only she could see. Trauma had hollowed her expression.

Tamas entered quietly with a tray. "You haven't eaten since last night. Please have something."

Vinny whispered faintly, "A building…collapsing." "What?"

"In that city, there was a very tall building. On the top floor, they lived. Every evening, they would sit in their balcony for hours…talking."

She swallowed.

"Below them, couples drove along the highway - on dates, to the cinema, on trips. But it never mattered to them. They were happy just in each other's presence. It was enough. For them."

Tamas frowned softly. "Who are you talking about?"

"The ideal couple," she said, her voice breaking. "The one we could never become. Because of me."

Tamas let out a quiet sigh, watching his mother unravel before him.

Nancy and Vanessa walked toward their car. Vanessa carried a bag stuffed with beer cans.

"This stock should last us many days," Vanessa said.

Nancy smirked. "At this rate, it'll be finished on the way."

Across the lot, inside another car, Damian sat watching them. He only wanted to see Nancy once more before she left.

Tamas lay asleep in his bed. The door creaked open.

Damian stepped inside silently…a dagger in his hand. He moved closer.

And stabbed him.

The vision shattered.

Damian blinked and inhaled sharply.

Vanessa drove with one hand on the wheel and the other holding an open beer can. Nancy sat beside her, equally intoxicated, the city blurring past them.

"I want to confess something," Vanessa said. "I sinned yesterday."

Nancy turned slowly. "When did you even get time to sin yesterday?"

"Last night. When you stepped out."

Nancy sighed. "So now I have to become your babysitter? Stay beside you all the time or you might sin?"

"I'm sorry. It won't happen again." "What did you do?"

"I stole a painting."

Nancy frowned. "A painting?"

"Yes. I saw a banner about an exhibition. I went there at night…and one painting just felt irresistible."

"Vanessa, we are not supposed to steal. In God's eyes, that's a serious crime."

"I know. I knew. But my emotions overpowered me." "What was so special about it?"

Vanessa's voice softened. "I had a friend. She loved art. A true connoisseur. She would have adored that painting."

"Is she dead?"

Vanessa quickly composed herself. "No. I'm going to give it to her."

Nancy studied her for a moment. "Alright."

After a pause, Vanessa glanced sideways. "You're unusually hurt by yesterday's failure. As if your life depended on it."

Nancy looked ahead at the road. "After this mission succeeds, God will retire me."

Vanessa's eyes widened. "Really?" "Yes."

"I've never heard of an angel retiring."

Nancy gave a faint, tired smile. "Some things happen for the first time. He wants me to pass on the light to newcomers like you. Consider it a reward for my services."

Tamas caught up with Eashna as she walked toward her hostel under the dim streetlights.

"Hi," he said casually.

She stopped and turned sharply. "You again? What did I tell you yesterday? Stop following me."

"And that you don't want to be friends with me," "Exactly."

"Fine," he said with a shrug. "But I can still be your bodyguard. You walk alone from your store to the hostel every night. It's unsafe. So I'll escort you safely."

Eashna crossed her arms. "If a group attacks us on an empty road at night, I doubt the two of us can fight them off."

"You're saying that because you don't know me," Tamas said confidently. "I'm a valuable asset of a powerful entity. He won't let me die so easily."

She raised an eyebrow. "Oh really? As if that entity is omnipresent and will instantly know when you're attacked. That's just an excuse to spend time with me."

"I'm not lying. You'll realize it sooner or later."

She stepped closer. "Let's assume you can protect me from others. How will you protect me from myself? I am my own assassin."

"What does that mean?"

Without another word, Eashna pulled out a blade and sliced her palm.

"What the hell did you just do?!" Tamas shouted. "Why would you cut your hand?"

She laughed. "If I scream for help right now, the residents in this area will beat you before the police even arrive."

"You're not actually going to do that…are you?"

"Yes," she said coldly. "Because I want to see how that powerful entity saves you."

Tamas panicked. "I was joking, okay?" "Now you're talking sense."

"You're insane."

She smiled. "I'll take that as a compliment."

Tamas grabbed her wrist, examining the wound. "You're bleeding a lot. We need a dispensary."

"Relax. A medical store will do." "But the cut could be deep."

Eashna rolled up her sleeves. Several similar scars lined her arm.

"I'm experienced," she said. "I know exactly how deep to cut."

Tamas stared at her. "You sound like a chef bragging about her vegetable-chopping skills."

She laughed.

Under the dim neon cross of a roadside pharmacy, Tamas carefully wrapped a bandage around Eashna's bleeding palm. She watched him quietly as they began walking again.

"So," she asked, "what do you think about me now?" "I think you're mentally…either ill or disturbed."

She laughed. "And you still want to be friends with me?" "Now I might have to reconsider."

She nudged him lightly. "Why do you care if I cut my hand?" "Because it's insane."

"Emotional pain is worse than physical pain," she preached. "So I distract myself."

"Like shopping malls during a sale? Buy one, get one free?" She rolled her eyes. "That's a stupid comparison."

"As if your reasoning is genius."

"Excuse me, it's valid. You wouldn't understand. What do you even know about pain?"

Tamas fell silent.

He had spent his entire life drowning in loneliness but he could not say that.

He only sighed. And reminisced.

Vinny sat alone in her room, drinking whiskey. A teenage Tamas stood at her door.

"Mumma, the walls of my room feel like they're closing in."

She didn't look up. "Am I the one drinking, or are you?"

"I'm serious. I can't stay alone anymore. I need people to talk to."

"You know that's not possible. Go back to your room and sleep."

Tears brimmed in his eyes.

Eashna and Tamas stopped at the gate of a hostel. "My hostel," she notified.

He nodded. "Yeah." "You went quiet." "No, I didn't."

"You did. When I said you don't know pain." "Really?"

She studied him for a moment. "Would you like to come in?" He nodded instinctively.

"My warden would throw me out."

"I'd gladly murder your warden for a few more minutes of conversation."

She smiled at that. "Bye, Tamas."

He waved reluctantly as she disappeared inside, leaving him alone once again.

The main door opened quietly. Tamas stepped in, trying not to make a sound.

"Where were you?"

He froze. Vinny was sitting in the dark, waiting. "I went out for a walk."

She kept staring at him, unconvinced.

Damian staggered out of a bar, visibly drunk. He dialed Tamas.

"Hello."

"Yes, Damian."

"How far has your story progressed with that girl?"

"If things go well, I think I'll be able to explode the Protection Spell soon."

Damian nodded to himself.

"To kill angels, you'll need a specific kind of dagger. I'll bring it to you tonight."

"Alright."

The call ended.

Damian opened his gallery and began deleting every photo he had with Tamas. His jaw tightened as he did it. When he returned to the home screen, a selfie with Nancy filled the display. Her presence in the picture steadied him.

The same rude uncle sat at his desk, irritated, shuffling bills.

Eashna approached hesitantly. "Uncle…" "Hm?"

"My salary was supposed to come the day before yesterday. It hasn't been credited yet."

He didn't look up. "Have you seen the work lately? Where am I supposed to bring money from?"

"But everyone else has received theirs."

"They have to be paid or they'll quit. You're my sister's daughter. You should understand."

"Yes, but we need the money at home."

"I already gave your mother money for expenses. Where did that go?"

"You know Papa has cancer. His medicines take everything." The uncle scoffed. "Then stop spending on his treatment.

He's useless anyway. Just lying at home all day."

The words hit her like a slap.

Eashna stood there, eyes filling with tears, her fingers curling into fists.

Damian and Tamas sat on the couch, glasses in hand. "Normally a man's biggest dream is to earn money," Tamas said. "But Jewel already sends us enough every week. We don't even have to work for it."

"She pays her clients so they stay satisfied and don't explode the Protection Spell,"

Damian replied. "It's in her personal interest. She doesn't actually care about any of you."

"That's not the point. The point is my dream." "And what is your dream?"

"First, to make that girl mine. Then to gain freedom." Damian nodded.

"You were going to bring the dagger, right?"

"Yes. Take mine for now. I didn't get time to buy a new one. I'll get another tomorrow."

"Okay."

"I'm staying tonight. You're about to fight a battle for the Devil. That deserves a party."

"Good idea."

"I brought your favorite whiskey." "Splendid."

The bottle was nearly empty now. Damian had taken off his coat and shoes and leaned back on the couch. Tamas lay sprawled across his bed, completely drunk.

"Why aren't you sleeping beside me?" Tamas mumbled. "Don't worry. I'm straight."

"First, I prefer sleeping alone," Damian said. "Second, after drinking, I don't trust the person next to me."

"You call me your son sometimes. And then you talk about trust."

"Aurangzeb imprisoned his own father."

"Excuse me? What trait of Aurangzeb do you see in me?" "You're the offspring of a cruel entity. The genes"

"You're the Devil's offspring too."

"No," Damian argued. "I am God's offspring. We were all angels once. When the Devil tried to rule Heaven, those who sided with him became demons after their defeat."

"So our choices make us evil," Tamas murmured. "Got it. I won't make such choices. Like today, I didn't."

"What didn't you do?"

"I wanted to meet Eashna. But you wanted to drink with me. Priorities."

"I appreciate that."

Later, Tamas appeared asleep.

Damian slowly sat upright. The drunken act faded from his face. He pulled out a dagger and approached the bed quietly. He raised the blade.

His hands shivered. He hesitated.

After a long moment, he lowered it.

He walked to the window, opened it, and stared outside. He looked ashamed.

"You won't be able to kill me." Damian froze.

"However, Nancy won't care if I die," Tamas continued. "Tell her my location. Let her kill me instead."

Damian slowly turned.

A blade pierced his stomach.

Tamas stood before him, fully awake, holding a glowing magical dagger.

Damian gasped.

Tamas twisted the dagger deeper into his abdomen. Where had he gotten it?

Damian collapsed.

Chapter Six

The Shape of Loss

Eashna walked back from work, slower than usual. The street felt strangely empty. No teasing voice. No footsteps behind her.

She glanced back once. Twice. Nothing.

For a brief second, disappointment flickered across her face before she entered the hostel gate. Maybe tonight…she had needed him.

She buried her face into her pillow and cried silently. Suddenly, a car horn blared outside. Then again.

Annoyed, she rushed to the window and pushed it open. Tamas stood below beside his car.

Before she could react, he pulled out the magical dagger and slit his upper arm.

“Oops!” he shouted dramatically. "Now we're similar." Eashna stared at him, stunned.

Then she slammed the window shut in his face.

Down on the road, Tamas remained standing in disappointment.

Sunrays struck Nancy’s face, forcing her awake. She opened the drawer beside her bed, pulled out a cigarette pack, and lit one.

Vanessa entered holding an envelope. “What’s that?” Nancy asked.

“No idea. Someone left it at the door. It has your name on it.”

Nancy frowned. “This place is a hideout. How would anyone know the address?”

Vanessa shrugged.

Nancy tore open the envelope. Photographs slipped out.

Damian’s lifeless body.

Her fingers quivered, but she forced her face to remain composed.

“Whose photos are those?” Vanessa asked.

Nancy swallowed. “Ah…God assigned me a secret mission. It’s

related to that."

"Oh."

Nancy crushed the cigarette under her heel and stood up. "Where are you going?" Vanessa asked.

"Washroom."

Inside, she locked the door.

And finally allowed herself to break.

She went on to cry unabashedly for an hour.

Tamas hurried to catch up with Eashna. "Why were you angry yesterday?"

"I wasn't."

"Then why did you slam your window shut?"

"You were honking outside my hostel and cutting your arm. Anyone could've been disturbed. If someone had seen you, they could've filed a police complaint. What did you expect? That I'd happily come sit in your car?"

"I wish," he said lightly. She sighed.

"By the way…how are you?" "Terrible."

"What happened?"

"The store owner isn't paying my salary. We urgently need money at home."

"Why isn't he paying?"

"He says the month was bad. No funds." "Oh." He paused. "How much do you need?" "Ten."

"Not ten lakhs, I hope?" "No. Ten crores."

He laughed. "Alright, take ten thousand from me. Return it when you get paid."

She looked at him carefully. "Are you sure?" "Of course."

"No. It doesn't feel right."

"Arey, I insist. If the money stays with me, I'll spend it on something stupid."

“I will return it to you when my salary comes.” "Yeah, no issues."

"Thank you."

“Problem solved. Just like that.” He smiled. “Now can you do something for me?”

She narrowed her eyes playfully. “You give a girl money and what exactly do you expect in return, Tamas?”

He laughed. “Not what you’re thinking. When’s your day off?” “Thursday.”

“Then on Thursday…can we sit peacefully in a nice café and talk?”

"I'll think about it."

Tamas smacked his head. Eashna laughed.

Nancy and Vanessa sat across a table, half-empty bottles between them, cards scattered under dim light. Nancy, visibly drunk, shuffled and dealt again.

“I think you should sleep,” Vanessa said. “You’ve been drinking since afternoon.”

Nancy smirked. “I don’t want to be an angel anymore.” “What?!”

She laughed dryly. “Nothing.”

Vanessa studied her. “Ever since you saw those photographs, you’ve been acting strange. They really were about a secret assignment…right?”

Nancy ignored the question. “Show your cards.”

Vanessa sighed and revealed them. “Three of a kind. Kings.”

“Seems like my bad time is starting,” Nancy muttered, dropping her own cards without looking.

She walked unsteadily to her bed. Curious, Vanessa peeked at Nancy’s abandoned hand, which consisted of an Ace, a Three, and a Seven.

Just then, Nancy’s phone rang.

She picked it up lazily. “Hello. Alright. That’s good news. I’m happy. Ash, I sound sleepy because I am…hmm. Okay.”

She hung up and returned to the table, pouring another drink.

“I thought you were going to sleep,” Vanessa said.

“It was Ash. The Devil’s offspring has detonated the Protection Spell.”

Vanessa frowned. "They called you. But not me. Again!”

“Stay with me. Complete missions properly. Maintain good behavior,” Nancy replied coolly. “When the time comes, I’ll recommend your promotion. Then you’ll get calls from God’s assistant too.”

“But others receive calls even before promotion.”

Nancy took a slow sip. “Some are special. The majority isn’t.”

She walked back to bed.

Vanessa remained seated, resentment quietly brewing in her eyes.

Jewel sat gracefully across from a forty-three-year-old man. Time seemed powerless against her; the Devil had clearly rewarded his most loyal servant.

“I fed my niece the apple,” the client said. “Just like you instructed.”

“Good job,” Jewel replied with a satisfied smile. “Your work will be completed soon.”

He hesitated. “Couldn’t we have used something else? I mean… giving chocolate to a child is much easier than convincing her to eat an apple.”

“We could have,” Jewel said calmly. “But I chose the apple deliberately. The Devil tempted God’s first creations with fruit. By doing the same, I mock God. And the Devil rewards symbolism. We earn extra points for that.”

The client nodded slowly, half impressed, half unsettled.

Clothes were scattered across Tamas’s bed. Shirts, jackets and jeans - each tried on and rejected in front of the mirror.

He finally settled on one outfit, adjusting his collar with nervous excitement. It was his first date, and he looked like any other inexperienced boy preparing for one.

Vinny sat on the sofa, eyes fixed on the television.

Behind her, Tamas tiptoed carefully, holding his shoes in one hand.

He moved toward the window, quietly slid it open, and slipped outside - avoiding questions.

The date awaited.

Tamas drove steadily, stealing occasional glances at Eashna beside him.

"Why are you working at a departmental store at this age?" "I'm studying too. Distance learning."

"Distance?"

"I only go to give exams. No need to attend college regularly."

"Interesting."

"You didn't know? Everyone knows." "I never attended college."

"Why?"

"We have our own business. I didn't feel the need to study further."

She nodded. "Oh."

"By the way, what does your father do?" Tamas asked curiously.

"Nothing."

"Then how does the house run?"

"We had a restaurant. The best in town. But my father got addicted to the stock market. He lost everything. Had to sell it all. After that trauma…he never worked again."

"I'm sorry."

"It's okay. I've accepted it. I work at my relative's store to support the family."

"And while working, you study too. Are you genuinely interested in studies?"

"No."

"Any business ideas?"

"They come to mind. But I don't have capital."

Tamas smiled slightly. "Once I finish this job for the powerful entity I talk about, we could start a business together. I have good investment money."

“Why would you make me your partner? I don’t even have money.”

“I would like to believe that you're intelligent. So, money’s mine. Brain’s yours,” he said confidently. “What say?”

"You trust me more than I deserve."

Vanessa drove carefully along the winding mountain pass while Nancy sat beside her.

“How long until we reach?” Nancy asked. “By evening,” Vanessa replied. “It’s far.”

Nancy lit a cigarette, the smoke curling between them.

“The witch we’re going to kill is named Jewel. Fifteen years ago, the Devil rewarded her with eternal youth for her work.”

“I’ve heard you need to murder at least a hundred people to earn that reward,” Vanessa said.

“You heard right,” Nancy answered coldly. “That’s why stopping her is necessary.”

After a pause, Vanessa glanced at her. “Yesterday you said you don’t want to be an angel anymore. Were you serious?”

“Yes. This war between God and the Devil will never end. I’m tired of duties and responsibilities. I want to be free.”

“Free? Meaning?”

“After this mission,” Nancy said. “I’ll request God to make me human.”

Tamas and Eashna sat across from each other in a quiet booth, menus pushed aside as they waited for their order.

“Have you ever been in a relationship?” Tamas asked. “Yes.”

“How many exes?” “Nine.”

He blinked in surprise. “That sounds like The Tale of the Nine Tailed.”

She laughed.

“How did the breakups happen?” he asked.

“Different reasons. But one thing was common. They all tried to restrict me. Don't wear this, don't go there, don't meet him. Endless rules."

Tamas nodded in understanding.

"What about you?" she asked.

"I've never been in a relationship." "Don't lie."

"I'm serious."

"But you're good-looking." "I just…never tried."

Vinny pushed open her son's bedroom door to call him for lunch.

Her steps froze.

His clothes lay scattered across the bed, carelessly abandoned. Tamas had forgotten to hide them back in his wardrobe.

A flicker of dread crossed her face. She pulled out her phone and began dialing his number.

But midway through, a realization struck her. Her fingers stopped.

The sky had begun to dim as Tamas drove Eashna back home. "Is there water in the car?" she asked.

"Yes. The bottle's right beside you."

"Oh." She picked it up. "Do you have a glass?" "Sorry. No glass."

"Oho. Drinking straight from the bottle never really quenches thirst," she said, though she drank anyway.

"My mom says the same," Tamas replied. "What do you think the reason is?" "Maybe psychological."

She hummed thoughtfully.

"One day I was very depressed," she continued, "so I wrote a poem. My first and last piece of art."

"Artists can be occasional," he smiled. "Go on. Irshad." She grinned and began.

Tamas stared at her after she completed. "Was that really original?"

"Yes. Why?"

"That's the best poetry I've ever heard." She laughed mockingly. "Come on."

“I don’t lie bhai.” “Bhai?” she teased.

“I mean…it’s a habit. I’ve never really been around girls.”

“Still, your confidence was sky-high when you approached me.”

“Confidence is innate to me,” he said with a grin. "Thanks for the compliment."

Chapter Seven

The Massacre Before Heaven Fell

A little girl, no older than nine, stood in the kitchen, her small hand gripping a heavy, pointed knife.

Her eyes were calm. Intentional. Not a child's eyes.

A song by The Doors played on the radio.

"The killer awoke before dawn. He put his boots on…"

She pulled a Halloween mask from her pocket and slid it over her face.

"He took a face from the ancient gallery…"

The masked child stepped into a bedroom.

The sound of repeated stabbing echoed in the dark.

"And he walked on down the hall.

He went into the room where his sister lived…"

Moments later, she emerged. A knife dripping red, and moved toward the next door.

"…and then he paid a visit to his brother...he walked on down the hall…"

Jewel parked her car outside the silent house, lit a cigarette, and stepped in.

She opened one room after another. Parents. Children. All dead in their beds.

A slow smile spread across her face, awed by the scale of the slaughter.

"Well done, my princess," she whispered. "Because of you, I can rise to the top of the witches' hierarchy. Where are you?"

She began climbing the staircase, searching.

Nancy and Vanessa arrived outside the slaughtered family's residence, tracking Jewel's presence like hunters closing in on prey.

They unsheathed their daggers and stepped inside. Upstairs, Jewel stood over the decapitated body of the possessed girl.

Downstairs, Nancy kicked the main door open and entered with Vanessa close behind. Their boots echoed against the floor. Jewel heard them.

Nancy moved room to room. In the first, a dead couple lay rotting on their bed. She winced at the stench and moved on. In the next, a stabbed child. She recoiled in disgust.

"What is this witch!?" she muttered. Vanessa gestured for silence.

They reached the staircase.

"I'll check the first floor," Nancy whispered. "Search the rest."

"Copied."

Vanessa cleared the washroom. Then the kitchen. Nothing. Suddenly, metal clashed upstairs.

Vanessa rushed toward the sound.

On the first floor, Nancy and Jewel were locked in combat, daggers flashing under dim light. Nancy bled - but less.

Before Vanessa could intervene, Nancy slammed Jewel to the ground and drove her blade straight into the witch's heart. Jewel's body jerked once…then stilled.

Nancy stood over the corpse, breathing heavily - victorious beside yet another fallen enemy.

Tamas slowly pushed the door open. Silence.

The hall was empty. He walked to Vinny's room and peeked inside. She was asleep.

He exhaled in relief.

Tamas sat at the table for breakfast. Vinny emerged from the kitchen carrying plates.

"What's for breakfast?" he asked. "Idli Sambhar."

"Nice. I was in the mood for something light."

As she served him, she asked casually, "Who is Eashna?" Tamas froze. “How do you know about her?”

“I asked first.” “She’s a friend.”

Vinny’s eyes sharpened. “So you detonated the Protection Spell.”

“No. She’s a demoness,” he replied quickly. “Now tell me, how did you find out?”

“You were gone the whole day without informing me. I got suspicious. So last night, after you slept, I checked your phone.”

Tamas nodded slightly. “Fair enough.”

Nancy sat alone on a rock, surrounded by whispering trees. In her mind, she was no longer an angel. She was human.

Free.

Damian ran ahead of her through golden light, laughing as she chased him in a game of hide and seek. Their laughter echoed carefree, untouched by war.

“Nancy.”

The vision shattered.

She blinked back to reality. “Huh?”

“I’ve disposed of Jewel and the family,” Vanessa reported. “Collected all demonic artifacts from her house. We can proceed to the next targets.”

Nancy nodded faintly. “Hmm.”

Tamas waited outside the departmental store until Eashna stepped out. They exchanged brief greetings.

“What happened? Why did you want to meet right now?” she asked.

“I need to tell you something.” “Go on.”

“My mother’s life is in danger.” He paused. “I mean…she’s very sick.”

“What happened to her?”

“Nothing serious. Just a little unwell.”

“You just said her life was in danger.”

“I’ve been watching too many TV serials lately,” he said awkwardly.

"Their dramatic language stuck to my tongue."

She chuckled. "You watch saas-bahu serials?" "My mom watches. I keep her company." "Okay…"

"So I came to say that I'll have to stay home for a few days to take care of her."

"Of course. Take care of your mom." "Thank you."

"You could've told me this over the phone, though."

"I won't be able to meet you for some days. So I thought…I should see you once."

She noticed the moisture in his eyes. "Tamas…are you crying?"

"No."

She wiped beneath his eye and showed him her finger. "Then what's this?"

"Oh."

She gently held his hand. "Go back to your mom. I'm not running anywhere."

"You never know." "What do you mean?"

He laughed softly. "I'm joking."

He pulled her into a hug. She stayed in his arms for a moment, comfortable, before pushing him back.

"Idiot, someone might see." Tamas blinked. "Sorry."

The angels' car descended from the mountains, cutting through sharp bends and drifting clouds.

Nancy sat in the passenger seat, cigarette between her fingers, her mood heavy and distant.

"Who's our next target? The mother?" Vanessa asked while driving.

"Yes," Nancy replied. "And then the offspring himself. We may have to follow traditional chronology…but the good thing is that they live together."

"So this mission will end soon?" Nancy exhaled smoke slowly. "Hmm."

Vanessa glanced at her. "And after that, you'll retire too?" "Yes."

"That would be the end of an era." Vanessa said, pretending to be emotional.

Suddenly, Vanessa's phone rang. She checked the caller ID and her face lit up.

"Why are you so happy?" Nancy asked. "Who is it?"

"For the first time, I'm getting a direct call from God's side."

"Oh. Congratulations." "Thank you."

"Pick it up then. Let's hear what they say."

Vanessa answered eagerly. "Hello, Ash. I'm brilliant. Why did you call me? You could've called her directly…Oh."

Her smile faded.

"What happened?" Nancy asked. "Where's your phone?"

"In my pocket."

"Why is it switched off?"

"It's not. It's malfunctioning."

"That's why they called me. Otherwise, they wanted to speak to you."

Nancy suppressed a laugh. "Give it here." Vanessa handed her the phone.

Tamas sat at the dining table, eyes fixed on the main door. The magical dagger rested against his waistband. He had been waiting all morning.

"Why are you sitting here since morning?" Vinny asked. "Just like that."

"Thinking about ideas for your book again?" "I could do that in my room."

She sat beside him, studying his face. "Then why are you here?"

"Mummy…please don't look at me like that." "Does it feel bad to lie to me?"

"What lie?"

"I know you detonated the Protection Spell. I read your chats carefully that night. That girl is human."

He sighed. "In this situation, I can't even say you shouldn't have invaded my privacy."

She laughed.

"Why aren't you angry?" he asked.

"I lost Gauransh because of my stubbornness," she said quietly. "My pride has always been my enemy. I want to treat you differently now…if we still have time."

The doorbell rang.

"Maybe it's already too late," Tamas whispered.

He hugged her tightly, then pulled out the magical dagger. "Go inside and lock the door."

"I'm not going anywhere."

"According to God's chronology, they can't kill me before you. So for me to live - you must."

"We can't kill angels, Tamas."

"I know. But I won't surrender without trying. Please." She stood up slowly. "I've stopped being stubborn."

"Good."

Vinny walked to her bedroom. The bell rang again.

Tamas approached the door and opened it carefully. No one stood outside.

He stepped onto the porch to check. Suddenly, the door slammed shut behind him.

He spun around and pounded on it. No response. He tried forcing it open but failed.

Spotting a brick in the garden, he ran to the window of his mother's room, smashed the glass, and jumped inside.

Vinny lay on the floor. Her throat slit. Beside her, another body.

Nancy. Slowly vanishing. Leaving for the dimension where angels and demons go after their death. A smile on her face suggesting she might reunite with Damian there.

Vanessa stood over the corpse, having killed her own partner. She spat on Nancy's face and fled.

Tamas dropped the dagger. Nothing no longer mattered.

He collapsed beside his mother, cradling her body, screaming in raw, unbearable grief as tears streamed endlessly down his face.

Vanessa stepped into her car and drove away as dusk swallowed the sky.

She lit a cigarette.

This time, the smoke failed to steady her. Tears slipped down her cheeks.

"This was for you, Anna," she murmured.

A memory unfolded.

Vanessa and Anna walked across endless green grass, wine glasses in hand.

"Now will you tell me why we're celebrating?" Vanessa asked.

"I got selected," Anna beamed. "As a patrolling angel in the Human World."

Vanessa forced a smile.

"You're not happy?" Anna asked softly.

"I am. For you." She paused. "But I'll be alone." "You have other friends in Paradise."

"You're different."

Anna squeezed her hand. "Once your training is complete, you'll join me. We'll be partners."

Vanessa's face lit up. "Really?"

"Of course." They hugged.

"We'll become the most successful patrolling angels in the Human World," Vanessa said with certainty.

Nancy stood in the balcony, smoking.

Anna approached. "Ash called. They've received intel that a demon legion knows our location. We should relocate."

Nancy chuckled.

"Running from demons would be cowardice. We're not going anywhere."

"It's God's order."

"Right now, I'm your direct superior," Nancy replied furiously. "And my decision is to stay. Let them come. We may never get a better chance for promotion."

Later,

Anna lay on her bed, whispering into her phone. "Ash himself called and told us to move," she said anxiously. "But she won't listen. Vanessa, she's my senior. What can I even do?"

A few days after Damian's legion murdered Anna, Nancy stood in a dock, facing a celestial jury.

A voice echoed from beyond view.

"Nancy, you are accused of disobeying God's order. Because of that defiance, your partner and junior, Anna, lost her life."

Nancy remained composed.

"God didn't call me that evening," she replied. "He called Anna. She never properly conveyed the urgency of the order. Perhaps she believed we could defeat a legion alone. A victory like that would have guaranteed promotion. She was ambitious."

A murmur spread across the chamber.

Vanessa hid behind concrete pillars at the underconstruction building, secretly watching Nancy meet Damian.

She had followed her.

Her eyes hardened. She dialed immediately. "Hello, Ash. I need to tell you something."

Damian drove through the empty highway.

Above him, Vanessa flew silently with her wings stretched against the dark sky.

Vanessa descended at the first-floor window of Vinny's house and knocked softly.

Inside, Tamas opened it, startled.

They sat at the edge of the bed, tension thick between them. "To get his love," Vanessa said, handing him the magical dagger, "Damian will kill you soon. You'll need this."

Tamas frowned. "But who are you? And why are you helping me?"

"I'm a demoness," she replied smoothly. "The Devil sent me. Damian betrayed him. The Devil wants him dead too."

Back in the present, Vanessa slowed her car after spotting a roadside eatery.

She stopped near a stall outside Burgers Brew and bought a pack of cigarettes.

A stranger nearby stared at her with unusual fascination.

"What?" she asked.

"Can I get one cigarette?"

She handed him one, along with her lighter.

"Your lighter is beautiful," he said. "It has beings from Heaven engraved on it."

"Keep it if you want. I was planning to change it anyway." "Why change it? It's good."

She ignored him and walked inside.

Vanessa ordered a burger combo and began eating. A bite. Some fries.

Suddenly, hiccups.

She drank cola. The discomfort worsened. Panicked, she rushed to the washroom.

Moments later, black blood spilled from her mouth in violent waves.

Her body trembled, and then collapsed.

Tamas stood at the edge of a terrace, hollow-eyed, ready to step into the void.

"Going to commit suicide?" a hoarse voice asked. He turned.

The man in the black cloak and hat who challenged God stood behind him.

"Who are you?" Tamas asked weakly.

"Should I say…the Devil himself?" he chuckled.

Tamas cried in despair. "Why are you here? To stop me?" "I don't wish to lose my most capable offspring."

"Me? Capable?"

"Yes. Because of you, we defeated God. Congratulations. You're free now."

"But the other angel is still alive." "She's dead too."

"How?"

"The moment she betrayed her partner Nancy, God stripped her of her angelic status. She became a demoness. Unaware of this…she went to a restaurant to celebrate." He laughed darkly. "Demons aren't allowed to eat."

Realization dawned on Tamas.

"You may now live an ordinary human life with Eashna," the Devil continued. "Your reward for helping me will reach you. The choice is yours. If you choose to live, I shall contact you again for my future endeavors against God."

And then,

he vanished.

Tamas stood alone at the edge, torn between the fall, and a fragile, ordinary future.